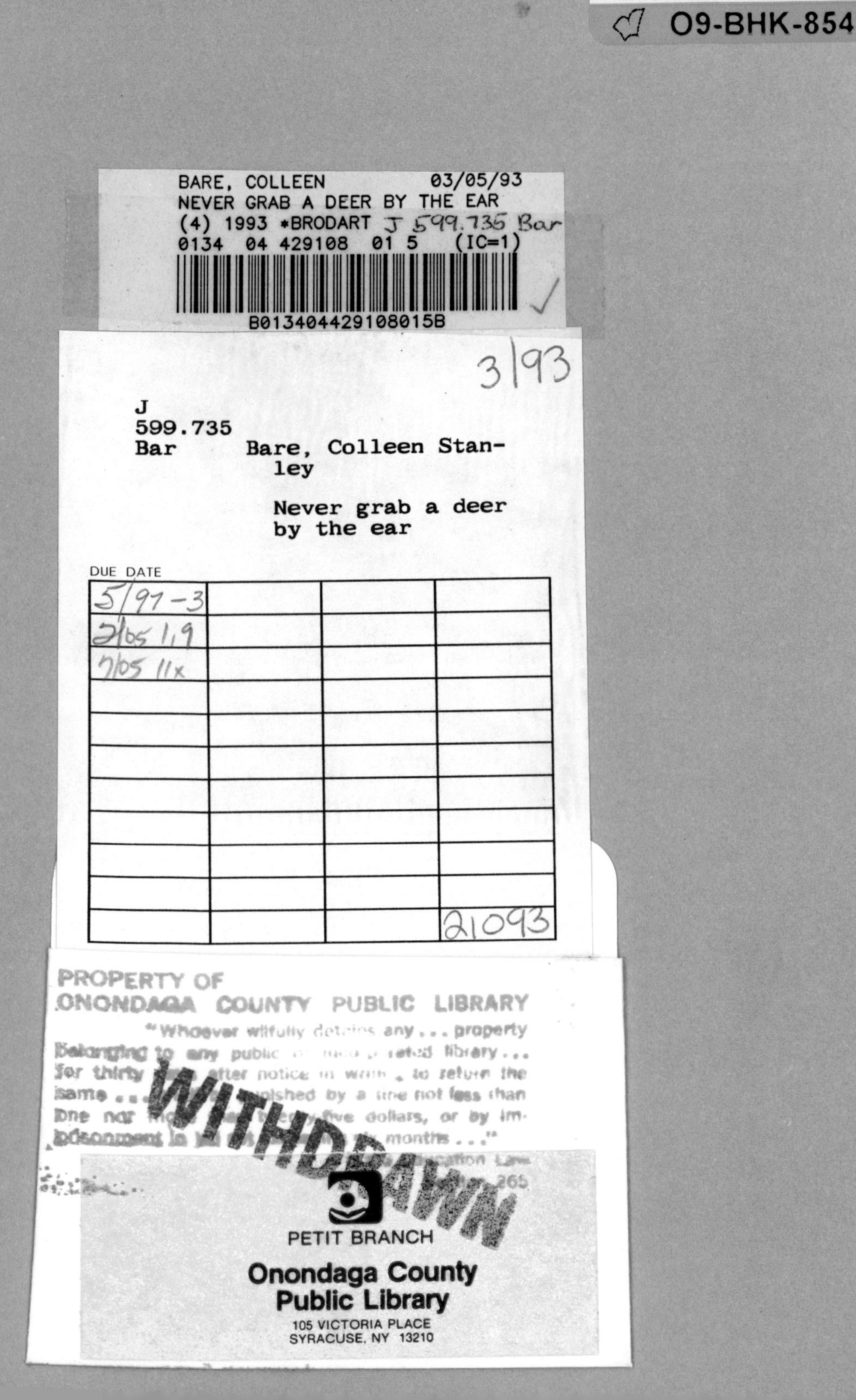

NEVER GRAB A DEER BY THE EAR

Photographs by the author

NEVER GRAB A DEER BY THE EAR

COLLEEN STANLEY BARE

COBBLEHILL BOOKS/DUTTON
New York

For Vernagene

Library of Congress Cataloging-in-Publication Data

Bare, Colleen Stanley.
Never grab a deer by the ear / Colleen Stanley Bare ; photographs by the author.
p. cm.
Includes index.
Summary: Describes the physical characteristics, behavior, and life cycle of the two native deer species in North America, the white-tail and the mule deer.
ISBN 0-525-65112-8
1. Deer—North America—Juvenile literature. 2. White-tailed deer—North America—Juvenile literature. 3. Mule deer—North America—Juvenile literature. [1. Deer. 2. White-tailed deer. 3. Mule deer.] I. Title.
QL737.U55B363 1993
599.73'57—dc20 92-7702 CIP AC

Published in the United States by Cobblehill Books,
an affiliate of Dutton Children's Books,
a division of Penguin Books USA Inc.
375 Hudson Street, New York, New York 10014

Designed by Charlotte Staub
Printed in Hong Kong First Edition
10 9 8 7 6 5 4 3 2 1

Never grab a deer by the ear, pull a deer by the tail, or pat an antler.

Don't even get too near a deer. Deer antlers can stab, strong slim deer legs can kick, and deer ticks can bite and make you sick.

If you see a deer, stay still and watch this beautiful wild animal. Deer are graceful, elegant, bright eyed, spirited, intelligent.

Deer can live almost anywhere. They are found in the mountains and at the seashore. They are in forests, meadows, swamps, deserts, near beaches and rivers.

Sometimes they are seen on city golf courses and in parks and gardens. Then humans get in their way.

On a golf course

Moose

Where in the world are deer? They are nearly everywhere—in North and South America, Europe, Northeast Africa, and Asia.

The deer family, called *cervidae* (sir-vi-dee), has about forty species, five in our country. These are elk, moose, caribou, whitetail, and mule deer.

Whitetail

Only two kinds, the whitetail and mule deer, are native to America. They date back a million years.

Whitetail deer roam much of North America. Mule deer (nicknamed "muley" for its big ears) are in the western part of the United States.

Mule deer

Wherever you happen to be, it is white-tails and muleys you are most likely to see.

Males, called *bucks*, weigh about 200–250 pounds.

Females, called *does*, weigh about 100–150 pounds.

Babies, called *fawns*, weigh seven pounds at birth. (*Does* is pronounced "doze" not "duz." Two does do, one deer does.)

Deer bucks are special because they have antlers.
Of all animals, only the deer family has antlers.

Cattle, goats, sheep, and antelopes have horns, but horns aren't antlers and antlers aren't horns.

Horns, made of *keratin* like finger-nails, are permanent.

Antlers, made of bone, grow in and are shed every year.

A baby goat with horns

A steer with horns

Bucks have antlers

A buck's amazing antlers grow in about four months, beginning in the spring.

They start from a bony base, as knobs covered with fuzzy skin called "velvet." The velvet nourishes and protects the antlers.

Soon the knobs look like clubs—

Then like a pair of slingshots.

In midsummer, the velvet-covered antlers are fully formed.

By autumn the velvet has peeled away, and the antlers are hard and shiny.

Now the buck is ready to use his antlers to push, poke, jab, and fight other bucks during the mating season. The winners then mate with the does.

After the mating season the antlers drop off. Rich with calcium, they may be eaten by other animals such as mice and squirrels.

The following spring or early summer the mother does give birth, often to twins.

Newborns can hear, see, and walk.

Their spotted coats blend with the surroundings to help hide the fawns from predators.

The does nurse their babies for three to four months, until the fawns can eat vegetation. By then, the fawns have shed their spotted fur.

What do deer do? They eat and eat and eat and chew and chew and chew. In early morning, late afternoon, and evening, they browse on plants, twigs, shrubs, grasses, leaves, herbs, and fruits.

Being *ruminants* (room-in-ants), like cows, deer rechew their food, called the *cud*. They spend their days lying in the shade, and lying in the sun, chewing and snoozing and snoozing and chewing.

A deer's thirty-two teeth may wear out in a sixteen-year lifetime.

Deer drink water, from streams, ponds, puddles.

Deer make sounds—barks, bellows, grunts. Mother does mew, their fawns answer by bleating, and all snort when startled.

Walk

Deer walk, trot, and can

Trot

run up to forty miles an hour.

So never try to catch a deer.

Gallop

Deer look silly, twisting and bending to wash their coats with their tongues. They scratch and bite at bugs and parasites like ticks, mosquitoes, lice, flies, and fleas.

Deer grow two coats a year: a heavy brown-grayish coat in winter, a lighter brown-reddish coat in summer.

Deer hide in brush and tall grasses, using their keen senses to watch, sniff, and listen for predators.

Deer enemies are:

humans—their guns and cars—
coyotes, cougars, bobcats, wolves, and wild dogs.

Winter coat

Summer coat

Does hide their fawns to keep them safe.

Deer use sight, smell, and touch to recognize other deer.

American deer have population problems. There are too many deer in regions where their predators have been destroyed by man. There are too few deer where drought and people have destroyed their habitats.

Perhaps deer should wear signs that say, "Do not disturb. Humans go away."

More Deer Facts for Young Scientists

Scientists have classified deer as mammals (Mammalia) because they are warm-blooded animals that suckle their young. Deer were placed in the order Artiodactyla because they are even-toed, and in the suborder Ruminantia because they have a four-part stomach and chew a cud. The deer family was given the name Cervidae, which includes nearly forty deer species in the world.

Two of these species are called native deer because they are found only in America. They are the whitetail (*Odocoileus virginianus*) and the mule deer (*Odocoileus hemionus*). Both kinds have many subspecies, including at least thirty for the whitetail and eleven for the mule deer. For example, blacktail deer are a subspecies of the mule deer.

Three other deer species live in North America as well as in Europe, Asia, Canada, and other parts of the world. These are elk (also called wapiti) (*Cervus canadensis*); moose (*Alces alces*); and caribou (*Rangifer tarandus*), also known as reindeer.

Index